BAKE THE SYSTEM

A SEASONED SLEUTH COZY MYSTERY, BOOK 10

GRETCHEN ALLEN

SUMMER PRESCOTT BOOKS PUBLISHING

Copyright 2023 Summer Prescott Books

All Rights Reserved. No part of this publication nor any of the information herein may be quoted from, nor reproduced, in any form, including but not limited to: printing, scanning, photocopying, or any other printed, digital, or audio formats, without prior express written consent of the copyright holder.

**This book is a work of fiction. Any similarities to persons, living or dead, places of business, or situations past or present, is completely unintentional.

CHAPTER ONE

Loretta Barksdale stared at the rising sun over the rim of her favorite coffee mug. She was seated on the shore of Breezy Lake. No matter how many times she had welcomed the morning from her favorite spot seated in her favorite chair, the sunrise never failed to take her breath away.

"Even after all this time, I still find magic in the sky when the sun rises and sets," she texted her best friend, Kelly Crenshaw.

"Didn't they have sunrises in Herring Heights?" Kelly responded.

"Of course they did," Loretta wrote back. "But they didn't look anything like this."

"You'd better take in all the sunshine you can," Pauline Pendleton called from the other side of Loretta's backyard. Loretta swiveled in her seat and stared as the older woman pulled on the dog leash in her hand. Nigel, her Pomeranian, yipped as they walked.

"Good morning to you, too. What are you doing here?" Loretta asked. In the time since she'd moved to Breezy Lake Retirement Village in northern Florida from her home in Herring Heights, New Hampshire, Loretta had often asked Pauline the same question. Pauline's excuse was always the same.

"I'm just out for a walk with Nigel. You know how he loves your yard," Pauline said. "It won't be long before we can't get outside at all."

"Why?" Loretta asked. "Is there some snowstorm headed this way I don't know about?"

Pauline threw her head back and laughed. Her artificially colored pinkish-red hair bounced with each giggle. "Snowstorm? We don't get snow here, but we do get hurricanes."

"Hurricanes?"

Pauline nodded her head vigorously. "I guess you haven't heard, then," she said with a grin. "Are you telling me that I know something Loretta Barksdale doesn't already know about? Has the earth shifted off its axis?"

"Will you please be straight with me?" Loretta

begged, quickly tiring of the conversation. "Is there a hurricane headed this way?"

"Have you not been watching the weather?" Pauline planted both hands on her ample hips. Her oversized floral frock billowed in the breeze.

"Are you only going to answer my questions with other questions?" Loretta asked. "Seriously. Is there a hurricane headed this way? How much do we need to worry about this?"

"Are you telling me you've never been through a hurricane before?" Pauline said.

Loretta shook her head. "Unless one slipped past me since I moved here, no. I've never lived in Florida before now. I've been through thunderstorms and tornadoes, but never a hurricane."

"I guess you better start paying attention to the weather," Pauline said, walking Nigel out of the backyard by his leash.

Loretta stood up from her chair. "Pauline, wait," she said. "What do I need to do? Is there a shelter we're supposed to report to? What's going to happen?"

"Try turning the news on for starters," Pauline called back as she walked toward the road. "Aside from that, you have a couple of days to prepare. Ask Kelly if you need more information.

"Pauline," Loretta cried. "Aren't you going to tell me anything about this? Like, what should I expect?"

"Expect to be inside. Expect to think your roof is about to get ripped off. And then expect days to clean up afterwards," Pauline said. "That's about all I can tell you."

Loretta continued to watch Pauline as she walked out of the backyard, hopeful she'd turn back around and give her more information about the impending storm. But Pauline continued, leaving Loretta to stand there in a stupor.

After a moment, Loretta picked up her phone and rushed inside to refill her coffee mug. She fired off a text to Kelly and searched through the couch cushions for the television remote. She located the remote and pointed it at the next-to-new smart TV mounted on her living room wall. She paid for a basic cable package each month, though she rarely watched anything.

Loretta searched through several channels before she found the local news. She settled down into her favorite reading chair and watched the screen. Kelly texted her back and suggested they meet at the coffee shop for breakfast.

"I'll meet you at the coffee shop in twenty minutes," Loretta responded. She set her empty coffee mug in the kitchen sink and hurried to her bedroom to change her clothes. She heard a low meow from the laundry room and rushed back out of her room and down the hall to check on Milo, her extra-large tuxedo cat.

Milo sat in front of the outside door staring up at the narrow window. He ignored her entrance into the room and opened his mouth again to release another low whine but remained stationary in his place.

"Milo," Loretta said. "What's the matter with you?" She reached down and scooped the large cat up in her arms, grunting slightly from his bulk when she stood upright again.

Milo wiggled himself free of her arms and jumped back to the floor. He resumed his sentry post in front of the door and meowed again. Loretta glanced at his food dish, which was shockingly still full. She reached above the washing machine and pulled out the cat food, shaking the bag for a moment. Milo didn't react at all.

"I don't know what to make of it," Loretta told Kelly half an hour later at the coffee shop. They were seated across from each other at their usual table. She circled the hot mug with her hands and concentrated on the steam rising from it. "I've never seen Milo behave this way. Not ever."

"It's the storm," Kelly declared.

"What do you mean? The hurricane is still two days off," Loretta said.

"It doesn't matter," Kelly said, shaking her head. "Animals can tell days before that there are changes coming. It must have something to do with the barometric pressure or something like that, but they can tell. I bet that's all it is. He's just reacting to the coming hurricane."

"Is it supposed to be that bad?" Loretta asked.

Kelly shrugged. "You know, it can be hard to tell what's going to happen until it actually happens. Unfortunately, hurricanes are like that pretty often," she said. "But I will say that a hurricane is a big deal."

"What should I do? I asked Pauline and she wouldn't tell me anything," Loretta said. She tried hard to keep the desperation out of her voice.

"The best thing you can do is board up your windows," Kelly said. "Make sure you have groceries for a couple of days and stay inside."

"Should we evacuate? Where should we go?" Loretta asked.

"I haven't heard for any calls to evacuate," Kelly said. "Which probably means the storm isn't going to be huge, but you can expect to get pounded with high winds and heavy rain for several hours. Even that can tear off roofs and break windows."

"Do we have a shelter here?"

"We can use the clubhouse if necessary and if it's really bad, sometimes the schools in the town over will open up and take people in."

"But nothing like a place for tornadoes?"

"Not here, but tornadoes after a hurricane are not uncommon," Kelly said.

"Wait a minute," Loretta said. "Are you telling me that after this hurricane blows through then we might have to deal with tornadoes as well?"

"Suddenly Florida doesn't feel like such a paradise, does it?" Kelly asked with a smile.

CHAPTER TWO

"You're worrying too much about this," Harold told her later that afternoon. They were seated on the deck outside of his house. Loretta enjoyed his remote corner of Breezy Lake Village. Shortly after Harold had taken the job as police chief for Breezy Lake Village, resigning from his post as deputy sheriff for Sunshine County, he'd purchased his own house on the lake tucked into a remote cove. He was known to everyone else as Chief Hargraves, but to Loretta, he was her significant other.

"You don't think I need to worry about boarding my windows up?" Loretta asked him.

"Oh, no, that's not what I'm saying at all," Harold said. "You do need to board your windows up. As a matter of fact, I'll swing by tonight and do it for you.

I have some extra plywood lying around here somewhere. I'll come by your house after I board up my own."

"But what about staying home or going to a shelter?" Loretta asked.

"Just pay attention to the news," Harold suggested. "If they're calling for anything larger than a category two hurricane, make plans to go to the shelter, but you'll want to bring your own food and water in case they run out."

"What do you mean, in case they run out?"

Harold nodded. "It's possible. It's also possible utilities might be down for a few days," he said. "Do yourself a favor and go home and pick up anything loose in your yard that could hit the house and cause damage. I'll come by and make sure the windows and doors are secure. After that, all there is to do is wait it out. No one is calling for evacuations yet."

Loretta stood up and leaned against the railing on the deck. She gazed across the still water in front of his house. "I don't know why this hasn't dawned on me before, but maybe moving to Florida wasn't the best idea after all."

"I'm surprised this is affecting you so much, Loretta," Harold said. He stood up and joined her at the deck railing. "You lived in Herring Heights your entire life. I know for a fact you have been through storm warnings before."

"I have, yes," Loretta said. "But blizzards are different in my mind."

Harold nodded his head. "I'll admit it takes some getting used to, but you're going to find out there's not a whole lot worrying will do to help. Do your best to prepare and then ride out the storm."

Before she could open her mouth to respond, her cell phone rang. She pulled it out of her pocket and glanced at the screen. "It's Pauline," she said. "Maybe she's decided to apologize for the way she spoke to me earlier today. She was very dismissive of my concerns."

"Oh, no," Harold teased. "I sure hope she's calling to apologize."

Loretta nudged him with her elbow and rolled her eyes at him before she put the phone to her ear and answered. "Hello, Pauline," she said.

"It always throws me off when you answer the phone knowing who I am before I tell you," Pauline complained. "I missed the days when phone calls were a mystery."

Loretta decided to keep her thoughts about the blessings of Caller I.D to herself. "What can I do for you?"

"You can bring your best dessert to the clubhouse tonight at seven," Pauline said brightly. "The Clubhouse Cooks are going to host a hurricane watch party."

"A hurricane watch party," Loretta gasped. "You want me to fix dessert for a hurricane watch party?"

Pauline cleared her throat. "I don't need to remind you that you are still part of the Clubhouse Cooks," she said. "Preparing food for an official club event comes with that privilege."

"Sometimes I wonder how much of a privilege it is," Loretta mumbled.

"Are you going to make dessert or not?" Pauline asked.

"I'll make dessert," Loretta said. "I hope a simple sheet cake is enough."

"A sheet cake is perfect," Pauline replied. "But don't make it too simple. We do want something that tastes good."

Loretta ended the phone call and shook her head. "I don't know how I get roped into these things," she told Harold. "Wait a minute! What about my windows?"

"Don't worry about it," Harold said. "I'll go ahead and board them up before I come to the watch party."

"But you still have your own to take care of," Loretta said. "Maybe I should just stay home and help you."

"There's no need to do that," Harold said. "As a matter of fact, why don't you go on home and figure out what you're going to make for tonight and I'll get started here. I'll swing by around five-thirty and pick you up for the dinner. That'll give me about an hour to board up your windows as well."

Loretta agreed and headed home. She thought about what she would make the entire short drive from Harold's house back to her own. At least Pauline didn't give her orders to create five separate desserts, which is something she had done before. She could handle a single sheet cake.

Loretta turned to her pantry to decide what recipe she would prepare. Despite the suggestion that she stock her pantry, Loretta had no desire to travel all the way to the grocery store. Anything she might need she could pick up at Johnson's Market less than a mile from her house. But she had made it a habit to keep her pantry well stocked for many years. It was a side effect of running her own restaurant.

After a quick perusal of her pantry shelves, Loretta decided upon a simple buttermilk sheet cake with caramel frosting. She moved her canisters to the kitchen island and began measuring out flour and sugar into a large bowl. She whisked in baking powder and salt then turned to the refrigerator for eggs, milk, and buttermilk.

Loretta melted the butter and beat the eggs then slowly added both to the dry ingredients along with the buttermilk, milk and vanilla flavoring. She mixed the cake batter just long enough to ensure there were no lumps and poured it into her large sheet pan. She set the oven at the correct temperature and waited while it preheated.

While the cake baked, Loretta turned to the stove top to make the caramel frosting. She began with more butter and melted it in the pan along with brown sugar. She measured in powdered sugar and then slowly added milk until the mixture boiled. Stirring constantly, she made sure the frosting did not burn. Once it boiled, she removed it from the heat and allowed it to cool. By then the cake was finished. She pulled the sweet-smelling cake from the oven and smiled.

"Perfect," she said to herself. "Nothing beats a homemade dessert like a buttermilk sheet cake." As soon as it was cool enough, Loretta spread the caramel frosting over the top and allowed it to set.

"What smells so good in here?" Harold asked when he arrived a little while later.

"Just dessert." Loretta swatted his hand when he tried to sample a corner of the sheet cake. "That's for tonight."

"I don't think they'll miss a little bitty piece of it," Harold said.

"You can wait like everyone else," Loretta scolded. "I don't think I've ever made dessert for a hurricane watch party before, though."

"Leave it to Pauline," Harold said. "Anyway, I'll be outside for a little bit. When I come back inside, we'll load up the cake and head to the clubhouse."

Loretta returned to her bedroom to dress for the dinner. While she fixed her hair, she could hear Harold drilling holes in the siding outside of her bedroom window. The inside of the house was suddenly much darker when she emerged, ready to go.

"It already feels rather gloomy around here," she observed when Harold joined her inside. "I don't know why but it feels like something terrible is about to happen."

"It's just the anticipation of the storm," Harold said. "Plus, the fact that I just blocked out all the sunlight."

Loretta held the sheet pan on her lap as Harold drove his truck to the clubhouse. The pan was large enough that she was afraid to leave it on the back seat without holding it. He opened her door and helped her down then walked around the back of the clubhouse to the kitchen entrance.

"Oh, that's just great," Pauline said, smiling. "That's a large cake. What kind is it?"

"Buttermilk cake with caramel frosting," Loretta commented.

"Perfect." Pauline really seemed to be in her element. "Just set it out on the dessert table like normal."

Loretta carried the cake out into the main dining area and placed it next to a pineapple upside down cake on the buffet table. Harold excused himself to make the rounds. As police chief, he was a popular guy just before a major weather event.

Loretta spotted Kelly across the room and headed in her direction. As she approached, she noticed two new faces. "Loretta, I'd like you to meet Dara Burke and her mother, Sally Snead," Kelly said, introducing Loretta to the women. "Dara and Sally just moved in."

"Oh, it's so nice to meet you," Loretta said, extending her hand to the younger woman. Dara smiled and shook her hand. Sally appeared lost in thought. Dara chatted easily with Loretta for several minutes while her mother wondered off.

"My apologies," Dara said a little while later. She eyed her mother as she spoke. Sally had made her way to the entrée table where she remained. "My mother is not much of a talker."

Dara was around Loretta's height and pencil thin. Her silver hair was piled on top of her head. Loretta guessed her to be in her late sixties. In contrast, her mother was a tall, round woman with short, dark hair sprinkled with gray. Her face was smooth and dewy despite her age.

"That's okay," Loretta said. "We're not always social around here, despite how it appears."

Dara shrugged and looked over at her mother. "She's almost ninety and her doctors say she's fine, but I think her personality has changed a lot in the last few years."

"Is that why you moved to Breezy Lake?" Kelly asked.

"Yes and no," Dara said. "We were living separately in Tampa until about a month ago. My husband died last fall and my mother was doing well at a care facility there, but the facility shut down last month and I just didn't have the heart to put her somewhere else new. I found this place to be the most affordable option for the two of us. I hoped she might make some new friends here."

"I bet she will," Loretta said.

Dara turned her attention back to the two of them. "Forgive me for asking, but are you two residents?"

Kelly immediately laughed. "The minimum age for residency here is fifty years old, but we are both qualified. As a matter of fact, I worked as the community manager at one time."

"And I moved here for the same reasons you did," Loretta told her. "I'm originally from New Hampshire, but when I found this place after a bad divorce, I decided I couldn't beat the affordability."

"The two of us are among the youngest residents," Kelly continued. "Aside from the police chief, Chief Hargraves."

"Is that the good-looking man standing over there by Clay Fulton?" Dara asked.

Before Loretta could respond, Kelly nodded. She leaned in and whispered, "That's Loretta's guy, which you'll soon find out. We have a very healthy rumor mill around here."

Dara laughed and shook her head. "I'm not surprised," she said. "Most retirement communities are thick with the gossip." She excused herself to check on her mother.

"I like her," Kelly said quietly after Dara left.

"I do, too," Loretta said. "She seems pretty nice."

"I worry a little bit about her mother, Sally," Kelly said. "I don't know if she's just in denial, but it's possible her mother is dealing with some sort of memory problems."

"Either that or she just doesn't want to disclose it," Loretta suggested. "We did just meet her."

"You're probably right," Kelly said.

Loretta scanned the room for Harold who had finished his conversation with Clay while they were talking. She spotted another unfamiliar face, a tall man standing in the corner alone. "Who is that?" she asked, nodding slightly toward the man, not wanting to appear obvious.

"Oh, you know what, I'm not sure," Kelly admitted. "I think he's another new resident."

"His name is Carter Sewell," Rachel Murphy said behind them. "I can introduce you if you'd like. I hear he's single."

Loretta turned around and faced the young community manager. "I think we're fine, thank you," she said. Rachel had proven to be a rather ill-fitting manager for the retirement community, but they'd begun to get used to her.

"We'll introduce ourselves," Kelly said.

Rachel shrugged. "Suit yourselves, but I think you'd like to talk to this guy. He's some sort of mystery author. Apparently, he's written a few books. Clay said he's rather interesting."

"And yet he's standing over there in the corner by himself," Loretta said ruefully.

"Just because he's an interesting guy doesn't mean he's necessarily sociable," Kelly said.

Rachel shook her head and walked away from them without another word. Loretta and Kelly shared a quick giggle. "Maybe we should introduce ourselves," Loretta suggested.

Pauline stepped to the middle of the room and clapped her hands together. "If I could have everyone's attention," she said. "The latest weather forecasts Hurricane Elvira will make landfall around three in the morning."

"Oh, that's early," a few people grumbled around the room.

"It is early, but that's usually how storms go," Pauline admitted. "Now, let's get this dinner going so the rest of us can get home and make any more last minute preparations needed."

"I'd like to make a statement," Rachel said from the back of the room, waving her hand over her head.

Pauline frowned but gestured to give Rachel the floor. "Ladies and gentlemen, our Community Manager has a few words to say."

Rachel smiled sweetly and stepped to the middle of the floor. "As soon as the storm subsides, I have hired a contractor to come in and take a look at the structures that belong to the community. I'm sure any of them can make recommendations for your individual homes, but just remember, the cost of repairs is on each homeowner individually."

Pauline stared at Rachel for a moment, then clasped her hands together in front of her. "Well, thank you for that," she said. Loretta was surprised at the level of sarcasm in Pauline's voice.

Loretta waited until the line had thinned around the buffet table. She walked up and filled her plate then took a seat near the front entrance where she, Kelly, and Harold ate their dinner together. Pauline had commandeered the television, playing a broadcast of a national weather channel to keep tabs on the impending storm. Loretta had a hard time tearing her eyes away from the radar maps as she ate. The only thing that distracted her was the sudden gusts of wind that seemed entirely too loud.

"I've never seen you so jumpy," Kelly said.

"Cut me some slack," Loretta said. "This is my first hurricane."

"Do you know how many hurricanes I've been through in my lifetime?" Clay asked from the other end of the table. "Because I've lost track. It's just something you learn to live with around here."

By the time dessert was served, only a few pieces of Loretta's buttermilk sheet cake remained. She plucked a small corner piece from the pan and set it on a plate then returned to her seat. Harold grabbed two pieces and followed her.

"I can't believe you got so much cake," Loretta said in a whisper. "You're not worried about saving some for the rest of us."

"I think the rest of us got there before we did," Harold said with a laugh. "Besides, if I can't enjoy a piece of my own girlfriend's cake, what is the world coming to?"

Loretta laughed and cut into her piece. She was pleased to hear a flurry of compliments on the cake as she left to head home for the evening. As she rode home the short distance in Harold's truck, her eyes were fixed on the sky above.

Harold dropped her off a few minutes later. He advised her to keep an eye on the news overnight.

CHAPTER THREE

Loretta's sleep was marked with periods of getting up and wandering around the house, looking out the small window in her door that wasn't boarded up and checking on the sky overhead. She could hear Milo wander through the house at times as well. By one in the morning, Loretta had given up on sleep. She stationed herself in the comfortable chair in her living room and turned on a local television station.

Hurricane Elvira had crossed over them at around two. At first, Loretta rolled her eyes at her own concerns. The wind and the rain outside her front door sounded a lot like a midwestern thunderstorm. By three, she realized her dismissal was a little too quick. She had experienced days of thunderstorm after thunderstorm before back home, but the sustained high winds and rain battering the side of her house made her feel trapped and restless.

Around five, the plywood Harold had affixed to her living room windows began to rattle with each wind gust. Loretta stepped outside into the garage and looked through the windows, the only others that had not been covered in preparation for the storm. She could see the sheets of rain falling in slants. Trees were nearly doubled over from the force of the wind. Instantly, she decided against driving her car down the road to the shelter. She would just have to ride out the storm within her own four walls.

A little while later, Loretta wrapped herself up in her bedspread which she pulled off her bed and carried into the living room. She was tempted to make a blanket fort in an effort to cancel out the noise outside. She was convinced that her roof was going to rip right off her house exposing the inside to the sky overhead.

The electricity was cut off at some point and Loretta did her best to maintain her sanity through the ordeal. She found herself pacing around the house, walking up and down the hallway from one end to the other. Milo took to hiding in the strangest places. At one point, she found him on top of the refrigerator. At another, he planted himself behind the toilet in the guest bathroom.

It was mid-afternoon before the winds finally died down enough that she could open her front door. The road in front of her house was littered with lawn furniture and other paraphernalia from her neighbors' yards. Loretta was grateful she'd had the forethought to remove anything loose and store it in the garage.

Harold knocked on her front door a couple hours later. Loretta pulled the door open and rushed into his arms. She was beyond grateful to see him in one piece.

"Are you alright?" Harold asked her when she released him.

Loretta nodded her head. "I can't believe that we made it through this," she said.

"Loretta, this wasn't a terrible storm," Harold said. "We really dodged a bullet here."

"Dodged a bullet? Are you kidding me? I thought my roof was going to get ripped off!" Loretta exclaimed.

Harold nodded while he continued to watch her carefully. "Your roof looks just fine," he said. "I'm sorry to say that you might be missing some siding on the east side of your house, but overall, your house looks fine."

Loretta inhaled deeply. She began to feel a bit of relief. The storm was over with, and she was still in one piece. She ventured down the hall to retrieve her cell phone. Kelly had already texted to check on her. Loretta quickly replied. "All is well here," she wrote. "Milo and I are in one piece. Harold is here to check on us right now.

She returned to the living room and gazed out the front door again. She was surprised to see a small panel van already parked a couple of houses up her road. "'Triple A Repair,'" she read then turned to Harold. "Contractors are already here, and the storm just moved out?"

Harold nodded. "Didn't you hear Rachel talk about it last night? She had already booked a contractor for community owned structures."

"Is that the way it's typically done?"

Harold shrugged. "That's a question I would pose to Kelly," Harold said. "I was just a sheriff's deputy the last time this area was hit with a hurricane. I didn't typically deal with that sort of thing."

"I think I'll drive over there and check on her," Loretta said.

"I doubt you'll be driving," Harold declared.

"I can't drive my car?"

He shook his head. "Too many downed trees in

the roadways. You'd be better off riding your bike down there."

"I think I'll walk," Loretta said.

"Or I can give you a ride," Harold offered.

"You don't mind?"

"Not at all," Harold said. "I'm headed that way anyway."

Loretta grabbed a few of her things and followed him out to the truck. She was surprised to already hear the hum of chainsaws in the distance. The air was still heavy with moisture. She climbed inside the passenger side of the pickup and rode silently around the lake to Kelly's house. Her gaze was fixed on the scenery around them. Harold skillfully dodged large limbs and tree trunks blocking sections of the road. Loretta spotted three more contractor vans on the way.

"Do you have your phone?" Harold asked her when he stopped in front of Kelly's driveway.

"I do," Loretta said. "I grabbed it before we left."

"Good," Harold said. "Just give me a call or a text when you're ready to go home and I'll come back by and pick you up."

"Thank you," Loretta said, opening the door to step out. She smiled at him before she shut the door and walked up the sidewalk to Kelly's house.

"I'm surprised to see you here," Kelly said when she opened the front door a moment later.

"If it's a bad time," Loretta said, halfway joking. "I can just get Harold back here if you don't want company."

"No, no," Kelly said, moving out of the way. "As a matter of fact, I am very glad you're here. I was just about to head out."

"Where are you going?" Loretta asked. She was more than a little surprised to hear of Kelly's plans to go outside.

"Door to door to check on my neighbors," Kelly said.

"Oh, that's a good idea," Loretta said. She wondered if she should have stayed home and done the same.

Kelly moved to the front hall closet and pulled out two yellow rain slickers. "You're going to need this."

"Are we supposed to get more rain?" Loretta asked, taking a raincoat from her. "Because the last I heard, the rain had moved out of the area."

"Trust me, you'll get plenty wet without it," Kelly explained. "There's enough moisture still in the air and rain on everything else that you will get soaked every time the wind blows."

Loretta put the raincoat on over her clothing. She

set her things down inside Kelly's front door and shoved her cell phone in her back pocket. "I'm surprised there isn't a committee set up to do this," she said as they walked toward the first neighbor to the left.

"There used to be," Kelly said. "Back when I was the full-time community manager, we had a committee set up to do this very thing, but Rachel dissolved that committee when she took over."

Loretta shook her head. She was not surprised to learn that Rachel had ended a useful function of another committee in Breezy Lake Village. Since taking over as the community manager, Rachel was not the most popular person around the lake. She had done more damage than good in the few months since she had arrived. Loretta was quite certain she wasn't the only one with that opinion.

Three houses later, Loretta began to feel even more at ease after the day long storm. So far, everyone was present and accounted for. She spotted a few more agile residents already out and about. By the time they reached the end of the block, Loretta was certain everyone had made it out okay. There was plenty of damage to several homes. She counted a half dozen homes in the first block with missing shingles. A few more homes sported broken windows where the homeowner had failed to cover the windows.

"Hey, look," Kelly said, pointing down the road. "I think that's Clay. I'm surprised to see him out and about."

"Why are you surprised about that?"

"Oh, I guess you didn't know," Kelly said. "Clay is one of those people with that specific kind of arthritis that's terribly affected by storms. I guess it's been a while since one has bothered him too much, but he's out walking around right now, so he must feel fine."

Loretta got a closer look at Clay and was instantly sure that he did not feel fine. His mouth was drawn into a tight grimace and his eyes narrowed when he saw them approaching. If he wasn't in pain, he was likely angry about something based on the look on his face.

Kelly must have picked up on it, too. "What's the matter, Clay?" she asked him as they approached. "You look like you're about to spit fire or something."

He shook his head. "Kelly, Loretta, have either of you heard from Rachel? We have a situation."

"I haven't heard from her since last night," Loretta said quickly. "What's the situation?"

"Kelly, have you talked to Rachel today?" Clay

asked, ignoring Loretta's question.

"No, not since last night, like Loretta said," Kelly said. "What's the matter? Is there something wrong?"

Clay sighed and dropped his arms to the side. He hung his head for a moment before he looked up at them again. "I have a disaster on my hands, that's what," he said. "I have two contractors who both claim they are the ones who Rachel hired to clear the roads. Both are demanding a deposit for their services, but Rachel is nowhere to be found."

"Was she planning to be here today?" Loretta asked.

"She was supposed to be staying here during the storm," Clay said. "She was set up in one of those rentals she insisted on having here after she started."

"Do we know that she was here before the hurricane hit?" Kelly asked.

"I visited her late last night before she turned in. She was here."

"Do you think she might have tried to leave during the storm?" Loretta asked. She looked up in time to see Harold turning around at the other end of the road. He headed toward them in his pickup. "Here's Harold now. Maybe we can ask him if he's seen her."

"I already asked him about ten minutes ago, but

maybe he's found out something." He turned and waited for Harold to park his pickup on the other side of the street.

"Have you found anything out about Rachel?" Kelly asked as soon as Harold stepped out.

He said nothing as he approached them. Like Clay, his face was drawn as well. "Harold? Is something wrong?" Loretta rushed to his side.

"I'm afraid something is very wrong," Harold said, nodding his head. "We found Rachel's car about a mile from the Breezy Lake Village entrance."

"Is she alright? Was she injured?" Clay asked quickly.

"No, Clay," Harold said. "Rachel wasn't anywhere near her car. I have a couple of my officers searching the area, but there has been no sign of Rachel. And by the looks of her car, she was either blown off the road or driven off in a hurry."

"What do you mean, by the looks of her car?" Loretta asked him.

"The car wasn't just parked on the side of the road," Harold said. "The front end of the car is buried in a small tree. It looks like she had an accident and then took off on foot."

"In the middle of a hurricane? Who takes off on foot in the middle of a storm like that?" Clay asked.

CHAPTER FOUR

Before Harold could answer Clay, the white contractor van with "AAA Fixers" written on the side skidded to a stop in front of his pickup. Harold had barely turned his body around to protest the driver's actions before a man jumped out of the van and slammed the door behind him. He stood about six inches taller than Harold. His long, gray hair was gathered in a ponytail behind his head under a ball cap.

"You," he said, pointing his index finger at Harold. "You need to come with me right now."

"I won't be going anywhere with you until you tell me who you are and why you're tearing around the roads in the middle of a retirement village after a hurricane," Harold said firmly.

"No, you have to come with me now, Officer," the man said. He wore a pair of navy blue overalls that zipped up the front. The name "Burt" had been stitched over the breast pocket.

"I'm Chief Hargraves, and you need to start by telling me your name."

"Fine. My name is Burt Oaks, and I'm the contractor your community manager hired to handle cleanup on the streets," the man said. "Only, there's another guy hanging around who claims he has the contract. So, you have to come with me and settle this here and now."

"This seems to be more up your alley," Harold said, turning to Clay.

"Oh, no," Burt said. He inserted himself between Harold and Clay. "I said you're coming with me now and that's the way it's going to be. I need the law on my side. I have a copy of the contract in my van if you want to take a look at it."

"Buddy, I'm going to tell you one more time," Harold said. "You need to stay out of my face unless you want your hands behind your back secured and a pair of metal bracelets. Got it?"

"I don't think you understand what's going on here," Burt said. "This other guy with Triple A whatever is going around with chainsaws cutting trees down in people's yards claiming he's authorized by the community manager. I know I'm licensed, bonded, and insured. Do you know if that guy is?"

"He does have a point," Clay said. "We often get hacks and scammers running around after storms. They like to take advantage of the residents by doing a little bit of work and then conning them out of a bunch of money."

"I understand that, but I still have the health and safety of these residents to worry about. We haven't even done a complete door to door check on everyone just yet."

"Can't you just do a door-to-door check where this guy is parked?" Burt interrupted.

"Yeah, whatever," Harold said at last. "If it gets you out of my face, let's just run down there and sort this out."

"What about Rachel?" Loretta asked as the men started to walk across the road.

"What about her?" Burt called back.

"Well, for one thing she's missing at the moment," Loretta said.

"I have a call in to the Sunshine County Sheriff's Department," Harold called back, reassuring her.

"Is there anything we can do in the meantime?" Loretta asked.

"Maybe call local hospitals and see if she walked in or something," Harold suggested.

"Can we get a move on now?" Burt insisted. "I'm sure Rachel will turn up somewhere."

As soon as the men sped away in their vehicles, Kelly turned to Loretta. "I'm going to continue knocking on doors," she said. "Why don't you stay here and call the hospital in Sunshine Falls to start with?"

"Is there more than one hospital there?" Loretta asked.

"There's just the one, but there are a number of walk-in clinics and urgent care centers."

"Okay, I'll start there," Loretta said. "Why don't you do the next four or five houses on this side of the street and then work your way back up here while I make the phone calls?"

"Sounds like a plan to me," Kelly said. "But if you find out something, whistle or wave your hands over your head or something so I'll know to come back."

"Same here," Loretta suggested. "If you need some help, just text me or something."

"What do we do if we find out Rachel was injured?" Kelly asked before she headed to the next house.

"At least if she was injured and she's in the hospital there isn't a better place for her to be."

"I hope that situation with the contractors doesn't turn into chaos," Kelly said.

After a quick search for the number, Loretta called the general information line for the Sunshine Falls Hospital. She waited while the operator connected her to the emergency room. She quickly explained to the receptionist who she was and why she was calling. The receptionist returned with her canned response.

"I'm afraid we can't divulge patient information over the phone," she said.

"I'm not asking for patient information," Loretta said. "I'm just looking to see if my friend checked in to the hospital. Like I said, local law enforcement found her car abandoned a mile from Breezy Lake Village. We just want to make sure she's okay."

"Again, I'm sorry, but I can't give you that information over the phone," the woman said.

"So, what should I do?"

"I guess you should wait for her to contact you," the woman said and hung up the phone in her ear.

Loretta held tightly to her phone to prevent herself from tossing it across the road in anger. She forced herself to take five deep breaths before she tried an urgent care center. She was met with the same response, although the receptionist on the other end was less snippy about it.

Kelly was still several houses up the road. Loretta scrolled through her contacts and tried Rachel's cell phone number. She had hoped someone else had already thought to do it, but decided it wouldn't hurt if she tried, too. Her the phone didn't even ring. It went immediately to voicemail. The recording informed her that Rachel's voicemail box was full.

"I can't get anyone to tell me anything," she told Kelly a few minutes later.

"You mean they won't even tell you if she's checked into the emergency room?" Kelly asked.

Loretta shook her head. "They wouldn't even tell me that."

"What do we do now?" Kelly asked.

"I think we leave it to Harold to make that phone call for us," Loretta said. "Either that or he can ask the sheriff to call. We just want to make sure she's okay."

"That's true," Kelly said. "I guess it doesn't matter who finds out as long as someone does."

"What do you want to do now?" Loretta asked. "I suppose we can head down the hill towards Harold's house."

"We're going to have to walk around a few trees in the road," Kelly said with a chuckle. "But I'm up for it. Are you?"

"Sure, why not?" Loretta said. "After all, what does one do after a hurricane but go for a walk?"

"They go for a walk and jump over a few hurdles along the way." Kelly laughed.

Loretta stopped walking a few minutes later. She could hear someone shouting in the distance." Do you hear that?"

Kelly stopped and listened. "It sounds like someone's yelling for their dog."

"No, I don't think they're saying dog," Loretta said. "It sounds like they're saying mom."

They exchanged a look and took off walking again, this time in quite a hurry. Half a block later, they met up with Dara Burke, the new resident they'd met the night before.

"Have you seen her?" Dara rushed toward them.

"Who?" Loretta asked.

"My mother," Dara gasped. "She's missing. She went missing sometime in the middle of the storm and I can't find her anywhere."

"Oh no," Kelly said. "I don't think either of us have seen her."

"Have you spoken with the police?" Loretta asked.

Dara shook her head. "I tried to call 911 but the recording said all circuits were busy," she said. "I didn't know another number to try."

"That's alright. I do," Loretta said quickly. She pulled her cell phone out of her pocket and immediately dialed Harold's number.

"I'm a little busy here, honey," Harold said when he answered a second later. Loretta could hear two men shouting in the distance.

"We have a missing person," Loretta said.

"Loretta, we can't declare her missing until it's been a little while yet," Harold said. "I'm sure Rachel will turn up."

"I'm not talking about Rachel," Loretta informed him. "Dara Burke is here. Her mother, Sarah Snead, has gone missing. She said she went out in the middle of the storm."

"Clay, I have to go," Harold said quickly. He mumbled something on the other end of the line that Loretta didn't quite understand.

"You can't leave," Burt shouted in the background. "I told you I need you here to sort things out with this idiot."

"I have a missing woman," Harold said angrily.

"She takes precedence over your squabble. Settle it yourselves or get out of this community. Those are your choices."

"I will sue your department if you don't handle this right now," Burt shouted. Loretta could tell that Harold had moved some distance away from him by the sound of his voice in the background.

"Where are you?" Harold said into the phone.

"Just up the hill from your house," Loretta said. "Dara is right here with us."

"Don't go anywhere," Harold ordered. "I'll be there in less than a minute." Loretta could hear the wail of his siren in the distance.

CHAPTER FIVE

Harold pulled up to where Loretta stood with Kelly and Dara a few minutes later. He cut the siren and exited his vehicle immediately. Loretta felt a shiver go down her spine when she noticed the look on his face. Her mind had been on Rachel and where she may have gone, but in truth, the situation with Sally was much more dire.

"When did you last see your mother?" Harold asked.

"Last night when we went to bed," Dara said. "It had to have been around eleven-thirty."

"When did you discover she was missing?" Harold asked.

"About thirty-minutes ago," Dara said. "I was up and down most of the night checking on the house. I guess I overslept this morning. When I got up, I realized Mom's room was empty."

"Is it possible she took a car or another vehicle?" Harold asked.

"No, my car was still parked in the driveway," Dara said. "My mother hasn't driven in ten years."

"Are you sure she went out in the storm?" Harold asked.

"Yes, there is no other explanation," Dara said, slightly annoyed. "I looked high and low in the house. She's nowhere to be found."

Loretta could sense the growing tension between Harold and the missing woman's daughter. She rested her hand on Harold's arm. "Does your mother have a history of wandering off?" she asked gently.

Dara sighed. "Unfortunately, yes. They tried to tell me that she has issues with her memory, but I think my mother is just older and quiet."

Harold and Loretta exchanged a look. "When your mother wanders off, do you know where she generally goes?" Harold asked. His tone of voice had changed slightly.

"Typically, she just wanders around the neighborhood."

"Can you send me a photo of your mother?" he

asked Dara and gave her his number. "The more recent the better."

"Sure, I can do that."

"We'll get her photo out across the village," Harold said. "In the meantime, I'd like for you to work with Kelly to canvas the neighborhoods and look for your mother. Will that work?" Harold turned to Kelly with a pleading look on his face.

"Absolutely," Kelly said quickly. Harold breathed a sigh of relief. "Since our current community manager seems to be missing in action, I'll make sure we get your mother's photo around. Then the two of us can go door to door looking for her."

Dara nodded her head quickly. "Thank you so much."

"I'll also inform the other officers and the county sheriff's department about your missing mother," Harold said. "I want you to know that this case takes priority for me."

"Chief Hargraves! Yoo-hoo, Harold Hargraves," Pauline Pendleton called out, interrupting them. She was headed in their direction at a fast pace, causing poor Nigel to rush behind her on his leash. "I need to speak with you immediately, Chief."

"We're a little busy here, Pauline," Harold said.

"I need to report a crime!" Pauline said adamantly.

"What crime is that?" he asked.

"Someone stole my lawn chairs from my front yard," Pauline said. She stopped in front of Harold and planted her free hand on her hip.

"Stole your lawn chairs? You do realize we just endured a hurricane, right?"

"I am quite aware of the current weather situation, Chief Hargraves," Pauline snapped. "And it's because of that hurricane that my lawn chairs were tied down. They didn't just blow away. Someone took them."

"Did you capture anything on your doorbell camera?" Harold asked.

Pauline shook her head. "No, the doorbell camera network was down in the storm. That means the camera didn't do your job for you this time. I want my property returned to me promptly."

"Here's what I want you to do," Harold said with a smile. "Go on down to the police station and file a report with the officer on duty. We will investigate your missing property in due time."

"That's not going to work for me," Pauline said. "I want you on this case right now."

"Pauline, we have a few more concerns of a little

higher priority to deal with at the moment," he said bluntly.

"Concerns like what? What could be more important than my missing property?" Pauline asked.

Before Harold could answer her, Brigitte Waldorf called out from the other side of the street. "There you are," she said to Pauline. "I'm so glad you found him."

"What do you want, Brigitte?" Pauline asked.

"I came here to report a crime," Brigitte said.

"That sounds a little familiar," Pauline mumbled under her breath.

"Chief Hargraves, someone stole my garden flag," Brigitte said.

"What is a garden flag?" Harold asked.

"You know that flag she flies outside of her front door," Pauline said. "I hardly think your flag was stolen, Brigitte. I'm quite sure it just blew away in the wind. We just had a hurricane, after all."

"Not true. Not true at all," Brigitte insisted. "I secured my flag before the wind blew. I'm a native of Florida, Pauline Pendleton. I know how to prepare for a hurricane."

"Ladies, ladies," Harold interrupted. "I will tell you just like I told Pauline. Please file a report at the police station. There is an officer on duty who will help you."

"I want you to look into this personally," Brigitte insisted.

"I'm a little busy with two missing individuals," Harold said. "One of which is a senior citizen in questionable health."

Loretta glanced at Dara as Harold spoke. A shadow passed over the woman's face, but she said nothing to contradict the police chief.

"I'll tell you what," Loretta intervened. "Why don't I walk with you to the police station and the three of us can look into things together. Will that work?"

A satisfied grin spread over Pauline's face. "That works for me," she said. She turned to Dara. "You'll soon figure out that Loretta Barksdale is a bit of a sleuth in her own right."

"Are you some sort of investigator?" Dara asked.

"Oh, no, no, nothing like that," Loretta said. "I've just had some luck figuring a couple of things out in the past. That's all."

"Stop being so modest," Brigitte said. "She's done more than just figure a couple of things out."

"Then maybe you can help me find my mother,"

Dara said. She glanced at Harold. "In addition to help from law enforcement, of course."

"Absolutely, I can do that," Loretta said.

"But what about my lawn chairs and Brigitte's flag?" Pauline asked.

"I'm quite sure Loretta can handle looking into all of it," Brigitte said. "Besides, a missing person takes a little bit more priority over what we've lost."

Pauline said nothing but cast her eyes downward. Loretta was quite surprised at Brigitte's words. She exchanged phone numbers with Dara and headed down the road with Pauline and Brigitte flanking her on either side. They headed toward the Breezy Lake Village police station where she hoped to file the reports quickly and then get back to the search for Sally Snead and Rachel Murphy.

CHAPTER SIX

Loretta found herself standing in front of the small counter in the tiny lobby of the Breezy Lake Village police station. Pauline and Brigitte stood on either side of her, with Pauline drumming her fingernails on the counter impatiently while they waited for the officer on duty to attend to them.

There was no mystery where the officer was at the current moment. Loud voices drifted into the lobby from the back of the building. Several men shouted over one another. Loretta was quite sure she recognized one of the voices as Burt, the contractor she had met earlier in the morning.

"I want this matter handled right here and now," Burt said.

"The only way you're going to know which of us

is telling the truth is to ask Rachel herself," another voice said. Loretta assumed it belonged to the second contractor.

"I want to know where your police chief has gotten off to," Burt continued.

"It's like we already told you," an unfamiliar voice said. "We're a little preoccupied with the hurricane that just went through here, not to mention two missing women."

"Conveniently, one of those women is Rachel herself," the other contractor said.

"Mr. Oliver, I don't want to have to remind you again," the female officer said. "Rachel Murphy's disappearance is a legitimate concern for us. Her car ran into a tree and was found abandoned."

"I still find it slightly suspicious," Mr. Oliver said.

"You just stick with that suspicion and see where it gets you," Burt snickered.

"I want the two of you to shut your mouths, sit down, and fill out the paperwork in front of you," the officer said. "Don't say another word to each other. I can have both of you escorted out of here if you keep it up."

Her words stirred up the argument all over again. Loretta cringed when she heard Burt insist that he was the one contracted by Rachel. Meanwhile, Donnie Oliver did his best to shout over him.

"I don't think we're going to get anywhere here," Brigitte said suddenly. "Maybe we should just go out and look for everything by ourselves."

"I want to file a police report," Pauline insisted.

"Why don't you stand here and wait to do that, then?" Brigitte said.

"Well, what are you going to do?" Pauline asked.

"Me? I'm going to walk around the village with Loretta," Brigitte said. "If I find my flag, great. But I think I want to help look for this lady. What was her name again?"

"Sally Snead," Loretta said. "I think you're right, Brigitte. We can look for your items as we walk around searching for Sally. I have to admit I'm quite worried about her."

"Fine, have it your way," Pauline said reluctantly. She headed directly for the door. "Are you coming or not?"

Brigitte rolled her eyes and cast a look at Loretta. They walked together to the front door of the police station.

"Can I help you?" Loretta turned around in time to see a flush faced young woman in a police officer's uniform approach the counter. "I've been a little busy in the back of the station."

"We heard as much," Brigitte said.

"Did you need something?" the officer asked.

"What's your name?" Pauline asked the officer.

"Officer Cates," the young woman said.

"Well, Officer Cates, we were just here to report some missing items we don't think blew away in the storm," Brigitte said. "But I think we are a little lower on the priority scale at the moment."

Officer Cates smiled slightly and nodded her head. She reached under the counter and produced two packets of paperwork and slid it toward them. "Why don't you fill out this paperwork and return it to me a little later," she suggested. "In the meantime, we are setting up a lost and found in the clubhouse dining room. You can check in there and see if your items have been found."

"That works for me," Brigitte said. She stepped forward and picked up both packets of paper.

"Are you going to be okay back there?" Loretta asked.

"I can handle them, Miss Barksdale." Officer Cates smiled.

"Oh, I didn't know you knew my name," Loretta said.

"Everyone knows your name around here," Officer Cates said with a knowing grin.

"I'm not sure how I feel about that," Loretta admitted to Brigitte as they left the police station.

"What am I supposed to do with this paperwork?" Pauline complained as they walked toward the coffee shop.

"I guess you could shove it up your nose," Brigitte said bluntly.

"Brigitte Waldorf, what has gotten into you?" Pauline demanded.

"Nothing," Brigitte said. "Actually, something has gotten into me. I guess I'm a little tired of complaining about small things when there are bigger fish to fry all around us."

"What are you trying to say?" Pauline asked.

"You and I being so worked up over a few missing items while people are missing is foolish," Brigitte said. "I saw Sally and her daughter Dara when they first arrived. Sally is quite a bit older than we are, but not that much. That could be you or me out there wandering around after a storm."

"Loretta, how are we supposed to find this woman?" Pauline asked. She said nothing in response to Brigitte's concerns.

"Right now, the best thing we can do is simply

walk around the village and keep our eyes open," Loretta said. She was grateful Pauline had decided to move beyond her missing lawn chairs.

"What do you think happened to Rachel?" Brigitte asked her.

"What I hope happened is that someone helped her after she wrecked her car," Loretta said. "I just imagine Harold will get a phone call anytime now telling him the sheriff's department located her in the emergency room at the hospital. Either that or she went home, and we just haven't found out yet."

"I hope you're right," Pauline said.

"There's my friend." Brigitte smiled. "I knew you were more concerned about Rachel then you let on, Pauline."

"You bet I'm concerned," Pauline said. "I don't know about you, but I don't want to have to break in another new community manager. It's bad enough we've had to put up with that young thing. I don't want to have to go through that process all over again."

"Pauline Pendleton," Loretta scolded. "What has gotten into you?"

"Now you're turning my own question around on me," Pauline complained. "Nothing has gotten into me. I'm just looking out for myself, and everyone acts like I'm a big jerk because of it."

"You're not a big jerk," Brigitte said. "There are just bigger concerns in the world right now, that's all. I mean, seriously, do you really think your missing lawn chairs hold a candle to two missing people?"

"Of course not," Pauline said. "I'm not a monster. I just believe Rachel will be found and she'll be just fine. And that woman, Sally, she probably just got lost in the storm and she's sitting somewhere waiting for someone to find her."

"At least we hope that's true," Loretta said. "Can we stop talking so much and start looking more?"

"Fine, fine," Pauline said. "Loretta, you take the left side of the road. Brigitte and I will take the right."

Pauline began to move across the road to the other side. Brigitte followed. A second later, Loretta heard the blaring of a horn and froze as a white van careened past them. The van was a blur as it raced down the road. Brigitte screamed and fell backward toward the road. She grabbed Pauline by the arm and pulled herself back in the nick of time.

Loretta rushed across the road to the two women. "Oh, my goodness," she shouted. "Are you two okay? Her heart raced in her chest.

"What on earth was that?" Pauline asked. Her hair hung loosely around her face.

Brigitte's face had immediately paled. She stumbled around for a moment wide eyed and disconcerted. "He nearly hit us," she cried. "I think I twisted my ankle. That man, the van. I can't believe how close that was."

"Did you see who was driving?" Loretta stepped closer and placed her arm around Brigitte.

"I saw them, but I don't know who it was," Brigitte mumbled.

"Pauline, can you call Officer Cates down at the police station for me?" Loretta asked. She tried to remain upbeat.

"Oh, now you want to talk about filing a police report?" Pauline asked.

"No, I'm not worried about a police report right now, but I think that we need some help. I'm not sure Brigitte is going to be able to walk the rest of the way."

Pauline's face registered understanding. "Oh, okay," she said. "I've got it now." She walked a couple of feet away and used her cell phone to call the police department.

CHAPTER SEVEN

"I think Brigitte needs to go home and rest for a while," Officer Cates said.

"Yeah, well, I think she needs to be checked out by a doctor," Pauline insisted. She was seated in the back of the officer's golf cart next to Brigitte. Loretta sat next to Officer Cates in the front with her body turned around to face the women in the back.

"I think you'll be lucky to find an ambulance anywhere close to here right now," Loretta said. "It sounds like some other areas were hit a little bit harder than we were by the storm."

"If you want to drive into Sunshine Falls to an urgent care center or to the hospital, I can certainly understand," the officer continued. "But I was a paramedic before I took this job here. I am more than happy to check her out again."

"Why don't you do that, Officer Cates," Loretta suggested. "If you can reassure us that she's okay, I think going home for a good rest will be sufficient."

"Why didn't you say you were a paramedic?" Pauline muttered.

Officer Cates ignored Pauline's grumblings. She turned off the golf cart engine and walked to the back. She pulled a pen light out of her uniform pocket and checked Brigitte over again. "Are you dizzy or light-headed, Mrs. Waldorf?" she asked.

"I am a little lightheaded, but I think it's just my nerves," Brigitte admitted.

"Do you think you need to go see a doctor?" the officer said.

Brigitte shook her head.

"Let's go back to your place," Pauline said. "But I'm not leaving your side."

"That's a good idea," Loretta said. "You stay with her for a while, and I'll continue looking around for Sally and some of your things."

"You should go by the clubhouse while you're at it," Pauline said.

"I will," Loretta promised. She waited as the police officer returned to her seat and started the golf cart up again. They headed around to the other side of the lake. Officer Cates skillfully avoided the downed tree limbs in the road as she drove.

"What do you know about Sally?" Officer Cates asked as soon as Pauline and Brigitte were safely back at Brigitte's house.

"Honestly, not that much," Loretta admitted. "I just met Sally and her daughter Dara last night at the hurricane watch party, just like I met you today for the first time."

"Point taken." Officer Cates chuckled. "I just wondered if you might have any insight to where she might be right now."

Loretta shook her head. "I have no idea where she might have gone," she said. "But Harold, I mean Chief Hargraves, and her daughter are out looking for her along with the former community manager, Kelly Crenshaw."

"What about Rachel?" Officer Cates asked. "I met her once when she started to interview me for my position with the department, but she ducked out of the interview pretty quickly."

"I think the chief and the sheriff's department have a good handle on the investigation into Rachel's whereabouts," Loretta said. "Don't you think we ought to be looking into that van that practically ran Brigitte and Pauline over just now?"

"Right, of course," Officer Cates said. "Why don't you tell me a little more about the description of the van again?"

"It's just like Brigitte and Pauline said, the van came out of nowhere. The only thing I'm sure about is the fact that it was white."

"And Brigitte mentioned the van driver was unfamiliar to her," Officer Cates said. "Did you get a good look at him?"

Loretta shook her head. "I didn't, but Brigitte said he was a bald man. Bald with a thick mustache that went down to his chin."

"Oh, no," Officer Cates said.

"What's the matter?"

"Bald with a thick mustache? That sounds a lot like Donnie Oliver," Officer Cates said.

"You think he was the one speeding past us?" Loretta asked.

"I think I need to put out a bulletin on him and the description of the van," the officer said. "Are you sure you didn't notice any lettering on the van?"

"Unfortunately, I didn't," Loretta said. "What are you going to do if he's found?"

"I'm going to get an official statement from

Brigitte Waldorf and Pauline Pendleton," Officer Cates said. "Along with your statement, I think that's enough to cite him for careless and imprudent driving."

Loretta rode back to the police station with Officer Cates. She wrote her statement about the van incident down for the officer, then set out on foot again. She was determined to do her best to find Dara's mother, Sally, despite the almost constant interruptions to her efforts.

Loretta had walked about a half mile from the police station when another golf cart slowed down behind her. She turned and smiled when she spotted Kelly behind the wheel.

"Did you give up walking?" Loretta asked.

"Not exactly," Kelly said. "It was Harold's idea for us to look around with golf carts. He took Dara in another one himself. That way when we find Sally, we can offer her a ride, unless we need to call for an ambulance, of course."

"You still haven't seen any sign of her?" Loretta said.

"Unfortunately, no, we haven't," Kelly said. "Where are your two companions?"

"Officer Cates and I dropped Brigitte and Pauline back at Brigitte's house," Loretta said. "Brigitte and

Pauline were with me until they were practically run down by a speeding van."

"You've got to be kidding," Kelly said. "What else can go wrong today?"

Loretta quickly shook her head. "That is not a question I'm comfortable asking the universe at this time," she said. "Let's not tempt fate."

"Why don't you ride around with me for a little while?" Kelly suggested. "I can't imagine it's comfortable walking over all of the branches and debris in the road."

"I can't imagine it's easy to navigate one of these golf carts around."

"You'd be surprised how good I am at this." Kelly laughed.

Loretta walked around to the passenger side and climbed in. Kelly took off again, driving slowly as she made her way around the large sticks and small branches that littered the road in front of them.

"Looks like someone's heading towards us," Kelly observed. She slowed down a little further and waited while the other golf cart approached.

"It's Rosalie," Loretta announced. She smiled and waved at her friend, the owner and operator of Johnson's Market. The market was located just a short distance from her own home.

"Good morning, ladies," Rosalie said. "It's nice to see you all survived the storm."

"How did you do?" Kelly asked her.

"Well, my house is just fine," Rosalie said. "I can't say the same thing for the market, though."

"Was the store hit hard?" Loretta asked.

"You might say that," Rosalie said. "But it wasn't the storm that did the damage. Someone took advantage of the storm and broke into my store and helped themselves to what they could find," Rosalie said.

Loretta glared at her best friend. "I told you I wasn't comfortable asking the universe what else could go wrong today."

"Oh, no," Rosalie said. "It sounds like the two of you made out worse than I did. Are your homes okay?

"We have two missing people," Kelly said soberly.

"Two missing people," Rosalie gasped. Her hands flew to her mouth. "Here I am complaining about a few missing vegetables and you're telling me two people are missing? Who are they?"

"Well, one of them is Rachel, the community manager," Loretta said.

"That young woman is missing in the middle of the hurricane?" Rosalie asked.

"Her car was found wrecked into a small tree

about a mile up the road from the entrance," Kelly explained.

"I hope they find her soon," Rosalie said. "Who's the other person?"

"She and her daughter just moved into the village a couple of days ago," Loretta said. "Her name is Sally and her daughter, Dara, is looking everywhere for her."

"When did she go missing?" Rosalie asked.

"Her daughter thinks she wandered out in the middle of the storm," Kelly said. "She hasn't seen or heard a word from her since."

"That poor woman went out in the in the middle of a hurricane," Rosalie said. "I hate to tell you this, but stories like that don't often end well."

"That's what we're all afraid of," Loretta said. "Although I don't think anyone has said that to her daughter just yet."

"Of course not," Rosalie said. "I think you're on to something there, Loretta. There's no need to ask the universe what else could go wrong today. Between my store getting burglarized, these two missing women, and the warring contractors running around, I don't know what's become of our village."

"What do you know about the contractors?" Loretta asked.

"Oh, you know those guys that show up to start fixing things as soon as the storm blows over," Rosalie explained. "I've seen two of them driving down the road yelling at each other. A couple of them acted like they were going to come to blows on the side of the road, and when they're not yelling at each other, they're throwing things at the other contractors already hired by residents. I just don't know what's gotten into people with this storm."

"This is unbelievable." Kelly shook her head.

"That's what I said," Rosalie said. "There's two of them I've seen running around making trouble with each other and then more trouble with everybody else. I really wish Rachel would be more careful who she hires to handle things around here."

"Rosalie, do you know the names of the companies of these contractors running around making trouble?" Loretta asked.

"Oddly enough, they both use the name 'triple A,' although one of them spells it out and the other one just uses the letters," Rosalie said.

CHAPTER EIGHT

"I'm not sure where to go next," Kelly admitted when they reached the entrance to Breezy Lake Village once more.

"Neither do I," Loretta said. "Have you heard anything from Harold and Dara?"

Kelly shook her head. "Not a word," she said. "At least not since we split up."

"Maybe they found something," Loretta suggested. "Maybe they found Sally and they have been busy getting her medical attention."

"I guess there's only one way to find out," Kelly said pulling her phone out. She typed out a quick message and sent it to Harold. "What should we do now?"

"I think we should head back to the police

station," Loretta said. "Maybe we can find out more information from Officer Cates. If no one has run across either Rachel or Sally, we need to know."

"I guess we'll head to the police station then," Kelly said.

"Why don't we stop in at the clubhouse and check for Pauline and Brigitte's missing things?" Loretta said when they were about halfway there.

"I think that's a great idea," Kelly said. "Maybe we can ask around a little more and see if anyone has seen Sally."

"What about Rachel?"

"Right, Rachel as well," Kelly said. She kept her eyes trained on the road in front of her.

They parked the golf cart and headed into the community center without speaking. For a moment, Loretta was concerned. She didn't suspect her best friend of anything, but it was odd to her that Kelly seemed much more concerned about Sally's disappearance than Rachel's.

"There's Clay," Kelly said once they stepped inside.

"Any news, ladies?" Clay asked when he approached them.

Loretta shook her head. "We've heard nothing on either disappearance," she said, eyeing Kelly as she spoke. "What have you heard? Any word from the police about Rachel?"

"That's right," Kelly said. "Someone was supposed to check with a hospital. Have you heard anything?"

Loretta breathed an invisible sigh of relief. Kelly did seem concerned about Rachel after all. Not that she would have had any opportunity to have harmed Rachel, anyway. Loretta just didn't want to believe that her best friend was capable of it.

Clay shook his head. "The last I heard, there was no sign of her at the hospital in Sunshine Falls or in any surrounding areas," he said. "I haven't heard any more than that."

"Like Officer Cates said, the hospitals and urgent care centers are probably going to be quite busy anyway," Loretta said.

"I know, but it would be nice if we could locate at least one of these missing women," Kelly said. "The more time goes by the more worried I get about them."

"Forgive me for saying so," Clay said. "But I'm slightly more worried about Sally than I am about Rachel."

"Why do you say that?" Loretta asked.

"Because even if Rachel was in a car accident,

she's decades younger than Sally," Clay said. "Can you imagine how difficult it would be for a woman of such advanced age to figure out where she is in the middle of a hurricane? They only just arrived here. She doesn't have any familiarity with the village yet. I hate to say this, but the circumstances surrounding her disappearance often end tragically."

"I know what you mean," Kelly said. "We are a village surrounding a large body of water. You take a woman in her late eighties that is clearly suffering from something along the lines of a cognitive disorder and put her out in the middle of a fierce storm in an unfamiliar area and you will often wind up with her washing ashore days from now."

"Oh, what an awful thought," Loretta said. "Let's hope that's not what happens."

"Nobody wants that to be what happens," Clay said. "But we do have to be open to the possibilities. Even though they'd just arrived, I know her daughter will need a lot of our support if that is the case."

"Of course," Loretta said. "Have you had a chance to talk to anyone else around here about Rachel or Sally?"

"That's actually what I'm doing right now," Clay said. "I told the chief I would stop in and ask around."

"I take it Harold and Dara haven't found any sign of Sally then," Kelly said.

"They haven't, at least not ten minutes ago when I last spoke with them," Clay said. "And unfortunately, no one around here has seen or heard anything from her, either."

"Have you asked about Rachel?" Loretta asked.

Clay nodded. "I asked about both of them simultaneously," he said. "With Rachel it's a little easier since most people know who she is by now."

"But still no one has seen her," Kelly said.

"No one has either seen or heard from her," Clay said. "If you'll excuse me, I have another matter to attend to."

"Let me guess, you have feuding contractors you have to go separate." Loretta chuckled.

"How did you know?" Clay asked, his eyes widening.

"We've been witness to their feud ourselves," Kelly said. "Plus, there are several other people that have been as well. Including Rosalie Johnson. Did you hear about her store?"

"What about Rosalie's store?" Clay asked.

"Apparently it was burglarized during the hurricane," Loretta said.

"Can this day get any stranger?" Clay asked,

throwing his hands up in the air. He turned away from them and headed back into the center of the large room.

"I wish people would quit asking that question," Loretta said. "I don't want to see the answer."

CHAPTER NINE

Kelly and Loretta continued to make their way around the lake. Shortly after they left the clubhouse, Kelly slowed down in the middle of the road when Harold and Dara approached in another golf cart. Loretta felt an immediate tug on her heart when she spotted Dara, whose puffy and red eyes spoke of her emotional state.

"I take it you haven't found anything," Kelly said softly.

Harold merely shook his head. "I'm afraid we're going to have to call in some support."

"I thought the sheriff's office had already been involved," Loretta said.

"That's not the sort of support he's talking about,"

Dara said. "It's okay. We've already had this discussion."

"I'm talking about an underwater diving team," Harold said. "Sunshine County has its own rescue and recovery team. Unfortunately, the emphasis will be on recovery."

"Oh, Dara, I am so sorry," Loretta said. "I know you were hoping we would find something out by now."

"This is a silly question," Kelly said. "But have you been back by your house? Maybe your mom was lost, and she found her way back there."

Dara shook her head. "We've been regularly checking the house," she said. "I highly doubt Mom has been back in the last twenty minutes."

"If you'd like, I can take you home," Kelly offered. "I'm sure Loretta won't mind running around with Harold for a while."

"Of course," Loretta said, stepping out of the golf cart. Dara simply nodded and walked around the front to Kelly's cart.

"I can't thank you enough for all of your help today," Dara said. "It's tragic to me that we had to get to know one another under these circumstances, but I'm glad to know all of you. Thank you for the kindness you have shown me."

Loretta said nothing but watched as Kelly took off again. Harold slowly began driving toward her house. "I thought we would go by and check on Rosalie at the market," he said at last.

"That's a good idea," Loretta said. "But first, do you want to stop by my house for some lunch? I doubt you've had anything to eat today."

"Why don't we stop by there after we check on Rosalie?"

"That's fine, if that's what you want to do, but Harold, I know you and I'm sure that you didn't sleep a lot last night. You're running yourself ragged today."

"We have two missing people," Harold said. "I'm afraid that can't be avoided."

Loretta said nothing more as they approached the curve before her stretch of the road. Harold slowed the golf cart slightly as they passed her house, but didn't stop. A few minutes later, Harold pulled over and parked in front of Johnson's Market. He shut the golf cart down and stood beside it for a moment. Loretta was still seated when she could hear the shouting in the distance.

"Tell me you hear that, too," she said.

"Yeah, sounds like those idiots again," Harold

said. He sighed deeply and walked to the edge of the parking lot.

"By idiots, do you mean the two contractors from earlier today?"

"That's exactly who I mean," Harold said. "Only I can't tell where the voices are coming from. Do you see anything?"

"I think I see a white van about a half mile up the road," she said. "Do you think that's them?"

"Probably," Harold said. He turned back from the road and headed toward the entrance to Johnson's Market.

"Aren't you going to go check it out?" Loretta asked.

"Eventually," Harold said. "Maybe they'll do us a favor and knock each other out before I get there."

"You really are tired," Loretta said. She had never heard Harold speak in such a manner, but she had to admit, it wasn't a terrible thought.

Rosalie Johnson met them at the door before Harold could raise his hand to knock. "I figured the two of you would have been up the road aways looking into that nonsense," Rosalie said.

"I think that noise is going to continue whether we're there or not," Harold said. "I thought I would stop by and check in about what's missing here."

"Oh, okay," Rosalie said. She led them through the store and mentioned several missing items. "I think the only thing they got was food."

"It's a little odd to me," Harold said after several minutes. "Typically, in cases of burglary during natural disasters, you often find people looting stores," he said. "Or at least causing as much physical damage as they do theft. But there doesn't seem to be that much missing, and I haven't seen any damage to the door or the windows."

"No, I don't think they broke in," Rosalie said. "The door was open when I got here to check on things this morning. My guess is the door blew open and someone just came in and helped themselves."

"Even so, I find it weird that they didn't take everything or at least more things," Harold said.

"I see what you mean," Loretta added. "You would think if someone was going to take advantage of the hurricane to steal from you, they would steal everything in sight. It's not like they were in danger of being discovered."

"I hadn't thought of it that way," Rosalie said. "But now that you mention it, it is a little odd to me as well."

"It's too bad the hurricane knocked out cell and Internet service," Loretta said. "We could have just checked the doorbell cameras across the road to see who helped themselves."

"I think we would know a lot more about everything we're looking into at the moment," Harold said. "We might even be able to trace Sally's steps with the help of those cameras."

"It's too bad about that poor old woman," Rosalie said. "But it's been so long I'm starting to worry about her wellbeing."

"You're not the only one," Loretta said. She glanced at Harold as she spoke. "The rescue dive team is coming in soon."

"Oh, that's terrible news," Rosalie said.

The voices outside seemed to grow louder. Loretta jumped when she heard a series of loud noises. "Was that gunfire?"

"I don't think so," Harold said quickly. "But I do think we need to go check out what's going on."

"Go on," Rosalie said. "I'll reach out to you if I need anything else. For now, I'm just going to contact my insurance company."

"Come and see me later if you need help cleaning up," Loretta said. Although there was little damage to the store, whoever stole food left a bit of a mess on the floor in front of the displays. Loretta followed

Harold back out to the golf cart. "Do you want to go back to my house and get my car?"

Harold shook his head. "I don't think we have time. Get in and hang on." He backed out of the parking lot quickly and headed down the road toward the noise. As they drew closer, Loretta thought the sounds were more like large pieces of wood slapping each other rather than gunshots.

They ascended the hill quickly. Harold slowed down a little when they reached the top. At the bottom of the hill, Loretta noticed two large white vans blocking the road. She could hear the voices shouting at each other, but the first van blocked her view. Both vans appeared to be rocking back and forth.

"Now what?" Harold said under his breath. He pulled the golf cart to a stop on the side of the road. "Wait here, Loretta. I don't need you in danger."

Loretta sighed and nodded. She watched Harold walk around the back of the van on the left. He disappeared on the other side, and the loud noises immediately stopped, but the voices continued to shout. Loretta decided to get out and walk around. She planned to stay close to the golf cart, honoring her word to Harold.

"I warned you already, Oliver," one voice

shouted. Loretta was certain she was listening to Burt Oaks screaming at his competition. She wondered what had started the bad blood between the two men.

"Get out of my way, right now," a voice she was sure belonged to Donnie Oliver screamed back.

"Knock it off," Harold's voice rose above the others. "I've already called for backup. The two of you are going to be under arrest if you say another word to each other."

On cue, the voices started up again shouting at each other. Loretta wondered how close Harold's backup might be. She was sure he was going to need it at any moment. She watched as the van closest to her continued to rock slightly. The noises had stopped, but the van continued to sway slightly back and forth. Curious, she walked closer to the van taking care to stay to the right side of the road.

A siren wailed in the distance. Loretta wondered if it was Officer Cates or members of the underwater dive team. Maybe it was neither and the Sunshine County Sheriff's Department had arrived. Either way, Loretta decided to head back to the golf cart before Harold caught her so close to the second van. She was still in the grass on the side of the road. She had hoped to catch a glimpse of Harold and the two men but made it only far enough to see the front of the other van.

She stopped and stared for a moment, surprised to see damage to the grill and lights on the front of the enclosed van. "I wonder if they had a little incident earlier," she mused. She could see streaks of red paint on the hood. Maybe the van had hit something aside from the other contractor's vehicle.

The siren neared them, then stopped suddenly. Harold reappeared around the back of the other vehicle. "Do you know where that went?" he asked her.

Loretta immediately shook her head. "I thought it was coming here," she said.

Harold shook his head quickly. "No, if it was for me, they wouldn't come with their sirens wailing," he said. "All I know is that it can't be good news."

Loretta exhaled deeply. She shook her head and raised her eyes to the sky which had turned a brilliant shade of blue with not a cloud in it. "It's amazing how bright and clear things can be after such a horrible storm," she said. "And I'm not talking about Hurricane Elvira either."

CHAPTER TEN

Harold decided to take her up on the offer to take her car to investigate the sirens on the other side of the lake. "Let's just leave the golf cart here for now," Loretta said, raising the door to her garage. The last thing she wanted was to be responsible for theft of a golf cart with so many other things going missing.

"I left my truck parked close to the golf cart kiosk," Harold said as he drove. "If you want to drop me off there, I can pick it up."

"Let's just worry about checking out those sirens first," Loretta suggested. "I don't care if you need my car for the rest of the day." She wanted to add that she had no intention of going anywhere. She didn't trust her luck with so many other things happening around her.

"Chances are, I'll be back by your house before long anyway," Harold said. "Depending on what's going on with the sirens, of course."

"Why do you say that?" she asked.

"Because I have no idea what those two knuckleheads are going to end up doing to each other," he said. "As it is, I probably shouldn't have left them alone, but right now, it's all about priorities and missing people are at the top of my list."

"Maybe we'll get lucky and they'll both decide to leave the village altogether." Loretta chuckled.

"Oh, I highly doubt that," he said. "They seem to be determined to duke it out right there in the middle of the road. And I doubt either one of them is going to volunteer to move their van first." He continued around the lake until he spotted an ambulance parked close to the marina.

"What are they doing?" Loretta asked when she spotted two paramedics pushing a gurney over the uneven grass.

"I want to say that they've found someone injured on the other side of the pier," Harold said. He parked her car and got out without another word. Loretta followed quickly behind him. Harold walked down the steep hill to the far side of the large pier right behind the medics.

"What's going on down here?" he asked.

"Sir, please step back," one of the paramedics cautioned him. "We have a report of a medical emergency."

Harold reached into his back pocket and produced his badge. "I'm the police chief here," he said. "Is there anything I can help with?"

The young paramedic's face blanched. "Excuse me, Chief," he said. "I thought you were just a curious onlooker. We had a call about an older woman wandering around down here."

Harold and Loretta exchanged a look. "Is she injured? We have a missing resident in her late eighties," Loretta inserted.

"I wonder if it's her," the paramedic said. Loretta followed Harold down the hill. They walked along the shoreline until they were within full view of the underside of the pier. The hill descended sharply leaving an almost cave-like expanse beneath the wooden pier on one side. As soon as the underside of the pier came in view, Loretta, Harold, and the paramedics stopped abruptly and stared.

"I guess that's where Pauline's missing lawn chairs went," Harold said.

"And Brigitte's missing flag." Loretta chuckled. Sally Snead was seated in one of the lawn chairs watching the lake lap the shore. She had created an outdoor living room beneath a section of the pier. She stared straight ahead at the water, apparently unaware of the approach of the paramedics until they were right by her side.

"Well, I guess that's one mystery solved," Harold said. He walked about ten feet back up the hill and pulled his cell phone out. Loretta listened as he informed a relieved Dara Burke that her mother had been found safe and well.

Sally quickly tired of the paramedics' attention. Loretta stepped forward and took a seat in the second lawn chair. "Sally, you don't know me, but we're neighbors," she said, extending her hand to the older woman. "I'm Loretta Barksdale."

"There was a storm," Sally said. Her voice was stronger than Loretta had expected. "I got caught in the storm."

"You did," Loretta said. "That's why these guys are here to check you out and make sure everything's alright. Why don't you tell me about finding the shelter while they make sure you're okay, alright?"

Sally nodded and sat back in her seat. She relaxed and allowed the paramedic to take her blood pressure while she spoke. "The lawn chairs were on the road," she explained. "It didn't take much to carry them down here. The flag sort of found me. It blew in my face, and I decided to hang it up."

"What about the turtle and rabbit down there?" Loretta asked, pointing toward the ceramic garden animals. She wondered who the animals belonged to and if they had been looking for them as desperately as Brigitte and Pauline had looked for their belongings.

"Oh, those things just sort of found their way to me," Sally said with a sly grin.

Harold descended the hill again. "Your daughter would like for you to ride along in the ambulance to the hospital," Harold informed Sally. "She said she'll meet you there, and I will follow along behind you."

"But I don't need to go to the hospital," Sally protested. "I'm just fine right here."

"Ma'am, you just survived a hurricane," the second paramedic said dryly. "Why don't you humor your daughter this time and let us take you to the hospital? You'll be back home by dinner time."

"Fine, fine," Sally said. Loretta wondered if she truly did suffer from cognitive issues. She seemed as sharp as a tack. Sally turned to Loretta. "Will you see to it these items find their rightful owners? It seems I have to go."

"I will absolutely get these items back to their

owners," Loretta promised. She squeezed the older woman's hand and smiled. "When all this is said and done, let's you, me, your daughter, and my best friend meet for coffee at the coffee shop. Sound like a plan?"

"It's a date," Sally said. She protested when the paramedics tried to put her on the gurney, insisting that she walk back up the hill instead.

"Can you take me to my truck, sweetheart?" Harold leaned in and asked her.

"Just take my car," Loretta said. "I'll call Kelly to come get me. That way you can follow the ambulance right away." She kissed him on the cheek and headed toward the road with her phone in her hand.

Kelly arrived less than five minutes later. "You promised to tell me what's going on," she said as soon as Loretta approached the car.

"The good news is we are down to just one missing person," Loretta said.

"Did you find Rachel?"

"No, we just found Sally," Loretta said. "She had set up camp beneath the pier on the open side."

"Was she alright? I just saw the ambulance leave," Kelly said.

"She was actually just fine," Loretta said. "They're taking her to the hospital as a precaution, but she was talkative and moving around. She had to get up the hill by herself and refused to get on the gurney when the paramedics tried to make her."

"That's a relief," Kelly said. She looked over the items Loretta had collected from under the pier and placed beside the driveway. "Are those what I think they are? Brigitte and Pauline's missing things?"

"That's exactly what it is," Loretta said. "I plan to let them know where to find their things."

"Why don't we just load them in the back of my Jeep, and we can run them by the house?" Kelly suggested. "Pauline is still with Brigitte anyway."

"Are you sure you don't mind?" Loretta asked.

"I don't mind at all," Kelly said. "And besides, that's one way to kill two birds with one stone. We only have to explain what happened once."

Loretta laughed heartily and picked up the lawn chairs while Kelly opened the hatch in the back of her Jeep. They carefully placed the lawn chairs, Brigitte's flag, and the other items in the back. "I guess we can just drop off the other items to the clubhouse on our way back to my house."

"Sounds like a good idea to me," Kelly said. "I don't know about you, but I'm okay with letting people find their missing items at the lost and found."

Loretta climbed in the passenger seat, and they

arrived at Brigitte's house a few minutes later. Kelly helped Loretta remove the lawn chairs from the back of the Jeep.

"Where did you find them?" Pauline asked before they approached the front door. She stood holding Brigitte's door open. "I take it you found the thief."

"Let's go inside and I'll explain everything," Loretta said. She set the lawn chairs against the wall on the front porch while Kelly carried Brigitte's flag inside.

"So, Sally is the one that took our belongings," Brigitte said after Loretta explained what happened.

"I don't know if she actually took them or simply found the items," Loretta said. "I wouldn't say she's a thief."

"I'm just glad the underwater dive team didn't find her in the lake," Pauline said. "Can you imagine what that would have done to the morale around here?"

"Morale? You're worried about morale when people are missing?" Brigitte said.

"I'm just saying it would not have been good for the residents of the community to know someone had drowned in the lake during a hurricane," Pauline said. "You can't blame me for being a little practical about these matters."

"I don't know what to think about you anymore, Pauline," Brigitte snapped.

"You know, I promised I'd get Loretta home," Kelly said suddenly. She shot Loretta a look.

"Yes, I would like to get home and put my feet up for a while," Loretta said.

"But what about Rachel?" Pauline asked.

"What about her?" Loretta asked. "The police are looking into her disappearance."

"I think the police are a little too occupied with other matters right now," Pauline said. "Loretta, you have to keep looking for her."

"I don't intend to stop," Loretta said. "I just intend to go home for a minute and get some lunch. And what other matters are the police concerned with?"

"She's talking about those two clowns driving around in their white vans," Brigitte said.

"The contractors?" Kelly asked.

"I don't think they're doing a whole lot of fixing," Brigitte said.

"They're doing more fighting each other than they are helping anyone around here," Pauline said. "If you look around, you'll notice you can still barely get around out there."

"I noticed on the way over here," Kelly said. "There's still a lot left in the road."

"We saw them less than an hour ago," Pauline continued. "They were out there on the road playing chicken. I swear they're going to get someone killed."

"I'll make sure to mention that to Harold," Loretta said. "He left to follow the ambulance to the hospital and meet Dara there."

"Kelly, if they do find Rachel alive, I sure hope you set her straight about how to handle these hurricanes from here on out," Pauline said.

"Pauline Pendleton!" Brigitte gasped.

"What? Someone has to say it," Pauline complained. "You need to tell her the right way to handle these contractors. We never had this problem when you were the community manager."

CHAPTER ELEVEN

Loretta burst out laughing as soon as she was safely back in Kelly's car. "I don't know what gets into Pauline sometimes," she said.

"Neither do I." Kelly chuckled. She turned around in Brigitte's driveway and headed toward the clubhouse. As she drove, she swerved here and there to miss debris still in the road.

"Oh, no," Loretta said as they drove.

"What's the matter?"

"It looks like something's blocking the way in front of the entrance," Loretta said.

"I see it," Kelly said. She glanced in the rearview mirror. "And I have someone behind me. I'm just going to drive up the road a little and turn around."

"I can't believe those two contractors are still at

it," Loretta declared as Kelly drove. They passed the entrance sign to Breezy Lake Village.

"I can't believe Pauline is so hung up on Rachel getting things right," Kelly said. She shook her head. "Pauline acts like the woman isn't still missing."

"I have to admit, I'm starting to get worried about her," Loretta said. "I'm worried something bad has happened."

"I was thinking the same thing, too," Kelly said. "I think she would have been located by now if we were wrong."

"I don't want to be right about this," Loretta said. She gazed down the road a way. She spotted something in the distance and pointed toward it. "What do you think that is?"

"I can tell you what that is," Kelly said. She slowed down as they got closer to the vehicle. "That's Rachel's car. It must have been towed or moved back here or something. I honestly don't know what they did with it after it was found."

Loretta felt her heart stop in her chest. "This is Rachel's car," she asked, staring out the window. "Kelly, that's a red car."

"You didn't know that Rachel's car was red? I guess you just haven't seen it up close," Kelly said. "What's the big deal?"

"Turn around," Loretta demanded. "We have to get back to the Village. We have to get back there and find those contractor vans. Go now."

Kelly said nothing as she turned the car around in the middle of the road. She sped back toward the entrance to the lake. "Are you going to explain to me what's going on or just let me drive like a desperate chicken?" she asked.

"I think I know what happened to Rachel," Loretta said. She looked around wildly for any sign of the white vans. "There! I see one of them." Kelly drove around a tree branch in the middle of the road and stopped behind the van.

"What do you want me to do?" Kelly asked.

"Call Officer Cates, call Harold," Loretta said, getting out of the car. "Call anyone but do it quickly." She walked around the side of the van belonging to Burt Oaks. She casually circled around the front and spotted the red paint on the hood again. Her heart sank lower in her chest.

The van moved again, swinging slightly. Loretta heard a light knocking in the back. She walked past the driver's side window and looked inside. There was no sign of the owner. She rushed around to the back and pulled on the door handle. The door was locked, but she knocked on it. Her knock was met with a loud knock. Someone was inside the van knocking rapidly.

"Kelly, come help me," Loretta said. She turned back to the door and pulled as hard as she could. "Check your trunk for a lug wrench or something!"

Kelly retreated to the back of her Jeep and returned with a crowbar a second later. "What are we doing?" she asked. "Why do you want to open the door?"

Loretta took the crowbar from her and pushed it in the small gap between the two doors in the back of the van. "There's someone in there," she said. "I thought something was strange earlier, but I was so concerned with everything else that I didn't check further into it. I thought it was just these two dopes tussling when Harold and I ran into the two of them in the road. But now I'm convinced someone is inside."

"Maybe it's the owner," Kelly suggested.

Loretta groaned as she pushed her body weight into the door trying to open it. "Knock on the door, Kelly," she said. "Knock on it and see what happens."

Kelly approached the van and knocked on the side. Her knock was met with a response. "Oh, my gosh," Kelly exclaimed. "You're right! There's someone in there." She joined Loretta trying to open the door with the bar.

"Hey, what are you doing?" Burt called from the other side of the road. Loretta stopped moving and looked over in a panic. "What are you trying to do to my van?"

"There's someone inside," Loretta said. "Help us get this opened."

"Get away from my van!" Burt thundered at them. "Get away or I'm calling the police."

"Just help us get it open," Kelly said.

"He's not going to help us," Loretta said. She stepped in front of Kelly. "He's not going to help us because he knows someone's back there."

"Get out of my way," Burt said. "You don't know what you're talking about."

"The police are already on their way," Kelly said.

"You better get away from my van. I'm getting out of here."

"You're not going anywhere," Loretta said. She rushed to the side of the van and blocked the driver door.

"Loretta, be careful," Kelly said.

"You don't know what you're doing," Burt growled. "But you're about to find out you made a big mistake, lady."

"We'll let the police figure that out when they get here," Loretta said. She gazed down the road past the large man. She could see Officer Cates headed in their direction.

"Be careful, or you might end up in the back of the van, too," Burt whispered.

"Be careful, or you just might wind up in jail," Loretta replied.

"You can't prove a thing," Burt said smugly.

"I can stall you long enough for that officer to pull up behind you," Loretta said. "And I can show her the red paint on the front of your hood."

Burt reached for Loretta and shoved her out of the way. She fell to the ground, landing on a broken tree branch. She could feel the sharp edge of a stick penetrate her leg above her knee.

Burt gripped the door handle and yanked on it just as Officer Cates stepped out of her car with her gun drawn.

"Stop right there," Officer Cates said.

Burt turned around slowly and raised his hands in the air.

CHAPTER TWELVE

"I can't believe Rachel was right here the whole time," Harold said later that night.

"Have you figured out what the motive was for him taking her?" Kelly asked. They were seated in Loretta's backyard. Harold had built a fire and Loretta moved the outdoor furniture in a circle around it.

"I can answer that," Officer Cates said. She had changed out of her uniform and was dressed in loose fitting yoga pants and a sweatshirt. "It turns out he met Rachel just outside of the entrance on his way in. Rachel said he arrived just before the storm had moved through. From what I gathered, she blocked his way and asked him what he was doing."

"How did he end up hitting her car?" Loretta asked.

"I suppose they got into a bit of an accident when she tried to stop him from coming into the Village," the officer said.

"But why was she stopping him?" Kelly asked.

"Probably because she knew he was up to no good," Officer Cates said.

"We don't know that for certain yet," Harold said. "But that is our working theory. As it turns out, Rachel had not made any formal plans with Burt Oaks. Donnie Oliver was the man she hired for the work around the Village."

"Burt Oaks planned to wait the storm out in the village," Officer Cates continued. "As soon as everything was said and done, he started knocking on doors. The sheriff will do a thorough job with an investigation, but from what I gathered so far Burt is a bit of a scammer. Especially when it comes to older people."

"Was Rachel hurt?" Rosalie asked she was seated between Pauline and Brigitte, who were uncharacteristically quiet.

Harold shook his head. "Thankfully, no," he said. "Aside from being very hungry and a few abrasions, she was fine."

"That's not exactly true, Boss," Officer Cates said. "That woman was as mad as a wet hornet. I had to stop her from lunging at the guy. If I hadn't been there, I think she might have done him some real damage."

"You're awfully quiet, Pauline," Kelly said.

"She's feeling rather guilty," Brigitte said.

"I'll thank you to keep your big mouth shut," Pauline said.

"Seriously, what's going on with you?" Loretta asked.

Pauline shrugged. "I guess maybe I do feel a little bad," she admitted.

"Why do you feel bad?" Kelly asked.

"Well, I was so worried about my lawn chairs after the storm that I never thought that Rachel might be right outside my door tied up in the back of a van," Pauline said.

"None of us thought she was right here," Harold said.

"Well, one of us thought that," Officer Cates said, smiling at Loretta. "I still don't know how you figured it out."

"It was the red paint on the front of his hood," Loretta said. "As soon as I saw Rachel's car was red, I put it together. I remembered seeing the van moving back and forth."

"It's a good thing you figured it out when you

did," Officer Cates said. "We still don't know what his intentions were with her."

"Let's just be glad we all survived the storm and came out in one piece," Harold said.

"What about Sally?" Kelly asked. "Did you hear anymore from Dara?"

"Sally was released from the hospital a couple of hours after she arrived," Harold said. "I think they more or less pushed her out the door."

"That's what I heard," Officer Cates said.

"What are you talking about?" Brigitte asked. "Are we talking about that shy older lady from the other night?"

"It turns out she's a lot feistier than you'd think," Harold said.

"That just goes to show you can't judge a book by its cover," Rosalie said.

"Or a contractor by his work van," Pauline said. She stared at the group when they broke out into a collective fit of the giggles. "What's so funny? It's true, isn't it?"

**

If you enjoyed Bake the System, check out the next book in the series, Dread and Berried, today!

AUTHOR'S NOTE

I'd love to hear your thoughts on my books, the storylines, and anything else that you'd like to comment on—reader feedback is very important to me. My contact information, along with some other helpful links, is listed on the next page. If you'd like to be on my list of "folks to contact" with updates, release and sales notifications, etc.… just shoot me an email and let me know. Thanks for reading!

Also…

… if you're looking for more great reads, Summer Prescott Books publishes several popular series by outstanding Cozy Mystery authors.

CONTACT GRETCHEN ALLEN

Visit my website for more information about new releases, upcoming projects, and be sure to check out my special Members Only section for extra freebies and fun!

Website: www.gretchenallen.com

Email: contact@gretchenallen.com

Visit the Summer Prescott Books website to find even more great reads!

Printed in Great Britain
by Amazon